Danny's Dream

Jack Gabolinscy
Karen Oppatt

NELSON
CENGAGE Learning™

Australia • Brazil • Japan • Korea • Mexico • Singapore • Spain • United Kingdom • United States

NELSON
CENGAGE Learning

Danny's Dream

Fast Forward
Silver Level 24

Text: Jack Gabolinscy
Illustrations: Karen Oppatt
Editor: Cameron Macintosh
Design: Ami Sharpe
Series design: James Lowe
Production controller: Seona Galbally
Audio recordings: Juliet Hill, Picture Start
Spoken by: Matthew King and Abbe Holmes
Reprint: Jennifer Foo

ISBN 978 0 17 012707 3
ISBN 978 0 17 012705 9 (set)

Cengage Learning Australia
Level 7, 80 Dorcas Street
South Melbourne, Victoria Australia 3205
Phone: 1300 790 853

Cengage Learning New Zealand
Unit 4B Rosedale Office Park
331 Rosedale Road, Albany, North Shore NZ 0632
Phone: 0508 635 766

For learning solutions, visit cengage.com.au

Printed in Australia by Ligare Pty Ltd
6 7 8 9 10 11 12 21 20 19 18 17

THE UNIVERSITY OF
MELBOURNE

Evaluated in independent research by staff from the Department of Language, Literacy and Arts Education at the University of Melbourne.

Danny's Dream

Jack Gabolinscy
Karen Oppatt

Contents

Chapter 1

The Skinniest Kid

Danny was short and skinny. His elbows stuck out. His knees were knobbly. His chest looked like a sack full of broken sticks. His friends called him Bones.

"If I were a chicken I'd be quite safe," he joked to his best friend, Eddy. "Nobody would cook a chicken that was this skinny."

"Ha ha ha!" laughed Eddy. "It doesn't matter. You're still my best friend."

Danny was the skinniest kid in high school, but the funny thing was that he ate more than anyone else. At the start of each day, his lunchbox was crammed full, but by the end of the day there wasn't a crumb left.

Danny was the skinniest kid, but he was also the most popular. He talked more and laughed louder than anyone. He told more jokes. He pulled more funny pranks.

But Danny wasn't always happy. Sometimes, when nobody was around to see him, he was sad. He was sad because he couldn't read and write as well as other kids. He was sad because he wasn't good at sports. He wished he was more like Eddy. Eddy was good at everything.

Danny tried hard to be like Eddy. He tried to play softball, but he broke a finger catching a ball. He tried basketball, football and volleyball, but he was too short and not strong enough. He tried everything, but he was never good enough and he always ended up feeling sad.

Chapter 2

The Marathon

One Saturday, the Olympic Games were on television. Danny watched the men's marathon. The runners didn't go fast. They just ran on and on forever. They didn't have big muscles like Eddy. They were more like Danny.

At the end of the race, the three winners got medals. They were all skinny guys with more bones than muscles.

"I'm like that," thought Danny. "I can't go fast. I can't sprint like Eddy, but I can run further than him. I don't get tired over long distances."

Danny couldn't forget the marathon race. He kept seeing it over and over in his mind. He even dreamed about it in his sleep. In his dream there was a short skinny guy behind the others. The short guy ran harder and harder, but no matter how hard he tried he couldn't catch up.

Then right at the finish, all of the runners sprinted for the line. They were all fast, but the short skinny guy was the fastest. As he ran across the line first, he lifted his arms up in victory. His head came up, too, and Danny saw that the short skinny guy was him.

The next day, Danny kept thinking about the dream marathon. He wondered if he really could run like that. He told himself not to be silly. It was just a dream.

But later that day, he said to Eddy, "I might run in the schools' cross country."

"Na!" laughed Eddy. "You stick to jokes and silly tricks. That's more your style."

A few minutes later, Eddy came back. "Hey! I've been thinking," he said. "You might be good in the cross country. You've got the build for it."

Chapter 3

Training

That afternoon, Danny started training. He jogged round the park three times. It took him nearly an hour.

At dinner his dad asked, "Danny, I saw you running round the park. What's up?"

"I'm going to run in the cross country," Danny answered.

"That's cool," said Dad. "I ran cross country myself."

"Don't overdo it," advised Mum. "A little bit each day. That's the answer."

At lunchtime the next day, Danny ran round the school grounds. Eddy ran with him, but after a while Eddy stopped. He bent over and put his hands on his knees.

"You go too fast for me," he puffed. "I'll see you in class."

After school, Danny jogged round the park again. Every day he trained – fast runs at lunchtime, long, slow jogs after school. Every night he dreamed his dream, and every morning he asked himself, "Do dreams ever come true?"

Chapter 4

The Race

Race day came. Runners from all the schools arrived at the stadium. Danny waited nervously for his race. His knees were shaking. He wanted to be sick. He didn't feel like a champion. At that moment, the dream had disappeared from his head.

Finally, they called for the senior boys. There were 109 altogether, and they were all bigger than Danny.

"Take your marks! Set! **Bang!**"

The runners started fast. Danny tried to keep up, but they were too quick. He fell further and further behind. He knew then that he couldn't really run. It had been a dream. And the dream had turned into a nightmare.

Halfway round the first lap, someone got tired. It was a big guy with muscles like footballs. Danny passed him. He felt like a switch had been turned on. All at once the dream came back and he felt good. He passed another runner. He lengthened his stride and passed two more runners.

By the end of the first lap, Danny was 84th. At the end of the second, he was 23rd.

"Run, Danny!" called his mum and dad, as Danny started the last lap.

"Go, Bones, go!" shouted Eddy.

Fifteen minutes later, a bunch of nine runners raced into the stadium. They were dripping sweat. They were breathing hard. They all looked tired.

Ten seconds behind came Danny, but he didn't look tired. He looked like he could run forever. He didn't see the crowds or hear them cheering. He just ran. He was living his dream. The others never had a chance. He raised his arms like a champion as he crossed the line.

Eddy jumped around as if it were he who'd won the race. "My mate Bones," he yelled, slapping Danny on the back. "You were great. You're a champion!"

Dad smiled proudly. "Good lad," he said.

Mum didn't say anything. She smiled and laughed and cried and blew her nose, all at the same time. Later she asked, "What's next, champ?"

"Food," grinned Danny. "I'm starving. Can I have something to eat please?"